Curious George®
Dinosaur Tracks
Jorge el curioso™
Huellas de dinosaurio

Adaptation by Julie Tibbott
Based on the TV series teleplay written
by Bruce Akiyama
Adaptado por Julie Tibbott
Basado en el guión para televisión escrito
por Bruce Akiyama

Houghton Mifflin Harcourt Publishing Company
Boston New York 2011

Library of Congress Cataloging-in-Publication Data is on file.

ISBN: 978-0-547-44960-9 paper-over-board
ISBN: 978-0-547-43888-7 paperback
ISBN: 978-0-547-55798-4 bilingual

Design by Afsoon Razavi

www.hmhbooks.com

Printed in Singapore
TWP 10 9 8 7 6 5 4 3 2 1
4500272162

Ages: 5-7
Grade: 2
Guided Reading Level: J
Reading Recovery Level: 17

Edad: 5 a 7 años
Grado: 2.º
Nivel de lectura guiada: J
Nivel de *"Reading Recovery"*: 17

George was curious about animal tracks.
He took photos of raccoon, frog, and
squirrel tracks.

**Jorge tenía curiosidad por las huellas de animales.
Tomó fotos de las huellas de un mapache, una rana y
una ardilla.**

"Wow!" said Bill.
"You have almost
every local animal except the fawn.
Come on! I'll show you where to find it."

—¡Qué bien! —dijo Bill—. Tienes fotos de casi todos
los animales de la zona, excepto del cervatillo.
—¡Vamos! Te mostraré dónde puedes encontrarlo.

A fawn is a baby deer.
It would make the perfect photo.

**Un cervatillo es un bebé ciervo.
Esa sería la foto perfecta.**

Bill took George to the place he saw the fawn.
"Good luck," he said. "After I finish fixing
the path, I'm going swimming in the lake."

**Bill llevó a Jorge hasta el sitio donde había visto al cervatillo.
—Buena suerte —le dijo—. Cuando termine de arreglar el camino,
iré a nadar al lago.**

George looked for
fawn tracks.
The first track he found was from a slithery
garter snake.

**Jorge empezó a buscar las huellas del cervatillo.
Las primeras huellas que encontró fueron las de
una serpiente jarretera que pasó deslizándose.**

Then he found duck
and frog tracks.
They both have webbed feet. That must be why they are
good swimmers.

Luego halló las huellas de un pato y de una rana.
Ambos animales tienen patas palmeadas. Seguramente por eso
nadan tan bien.

George saw that fish do not
leave any tracks!

¡Jorge descubrió que los peces no dejan huellas!

Then George found the biggest tracks
he had seen yet!
Could the tracks be from a giant snake with duck
feet?
George followed the tracks.

**Entonces, ¡Jorge halló unas huellas más grandes
que todas las que había visto!
¿Podrían pertenecer a una serpiente gigante con
patas de pato?
Jorge siguió las huellas.**

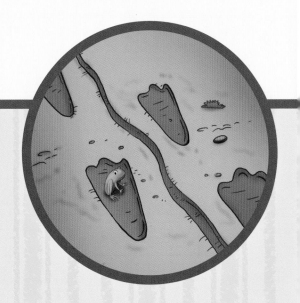

They ended at the
lake. George had an idea.
He had seen these tracks in a book.
They were dinosaur tracks!

**Las huellas terminaban en el lago. Jorge tuvo una idea.
Ya había visto huellas como esas en un libro.
¡Eran huellas de dinosaurio!**

He made a trail of food back to his house.
Maybe the dinosaur would come out to eat.
Then George could take a photo.

**De regreso a su casa, dejó un rastro de comida.
Tal vez el dinosaurio saliera a comérsela.
Entonces, Jorge podría tomarle una foto.**

But wait! George went home to look
at the book.
Some dinosaurs eat meat. Uh-oh.
Maybe they would eat him!

**¡Un momento! Jorge fue a casa a mirar en su libro.
Algunos dinosaurios comen carne. ¡Ay, no!
¡Podrían comérselo a él!**

George went
back to the water.
He saw the tracks were now
coming out of the lake!

Jorge regresó al lago.
¡Vio que ahora las huellas salían del agua!

The tracks were headed
toward Bill's house.
George had to warn Bill!

**Las huellas se dirigían hacia casa de Bill.
¡Jorge debía alertar a Bill!**

"I guess those do look like dinosaur
tracks," Bill said.
"But I made the tracks."

**–Supongo que sí parecen huellas de
dinosaurio –dijo Bill–.
Pero fui yo quien las hizo.**

"I went swimming with my flippers. I had my rake too."
George was happy that Bill left the tracks.
A hungry dinosaur would be scary!

—Fui al lago con mis aletas. Tambien tenía mi azada.
Jorge se alegró de que las huellas fueran de Bill. ¡Un dinosaurio
hambriento sería algo aterrador!

George still wanted a special photo.
The trail of food that led to the lake was still there.

Jorge aún quería tomar una foto especial.
El rastro de comida que iba hasta el lago aún seguía allí.

Suddenly, the fawn showed up to eat the food
. . . with the mama deer!

**De repente, apareció el cervatillo y empezó a
comerse la comida . . . ¡con mamá cierva!**

It was the perfect picture to complete George's collection—even if it was not a dinosaur!

Era la foto perfecta para que Jorge completara su colección, ¡aunque no fuera de un dinosaurio!

Animal Tracks

Look at the animals and their matching tracks.

What do you think George's tracks look like?

Making Tracks!

Did you know that you can make plaster casts of animal tracks? Next time you and an adult find an animal track while on a hike, in a park, or exploring your own backyard, try it—it's fun and easy!

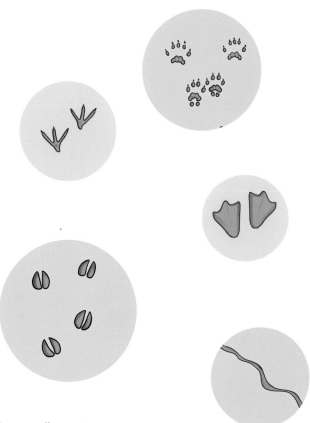

What you will need:

Plaster of Paris (found at craft stores), a bottle of water, plastic spoons, paper towels, a plastic container or paper cups to mix the plaster, a small trowel or something to dig with, paint, a backpack to carry everything in, and a grownup to help.

Making Tracks!

What to do:

1. Find a good, clean animal track in mud that has dried enough to keep its shape when you press on it lightly.

2. Lay out all your supplies. Pour about 3/4 cup of plaster into the plastic container. Quickly stir in water until the plaster is thin enough to pour, yet not too runny. Tap on the edge of the container to get out most of the air bubbles. Do this quickly, because the plaster begins to set within a few seconds.

3. Carefully pour the plaster mixture into the track. Let the plaster set for at least a half hour.

4. When the plaster is firm, carefully dig under the cast and lift it up. Take it home and let it dry overnight.

5. When the plaster cast is completely dry, clean it off with a brush. You may want to paint the cast.

Now you have an animal track that will last forever!